THE INCREDIBLE HULK

THE SECRET STORY OF MARVEL'S GAMMA-POWERED GOLIATH

By David Anthony Kraft

Featuring the art of
Jack Kirby, Herb Trimpe,
Sal Buscema and Klaus Janson

And the scripting of
Stan Lee, Roy Thomas,
Roger Stern and Peter Gillis

 CHILDRENS PRESS, CHICAGO

Library of Congress Cataloging in Publication Data

Kraft, David Anthony.
   The Incredible Hulk.

   Summary: Discusses the origin of the comic
strip character Bruce Banner, who, when faced
with danger or emotional stress, changes into
the Hulk. Includes several examples of his
adventures.
   1. Hulk (Comic strip)—Juvenile literature.
[1. Hulk (Comic strip) 2. Cartoons and comics.
3. Adventure stories] I. Kirby, Jack, ill.
II. Trimpe, Herb, ill.   III. Buscema, Sal, ill.
IV. Janson, Klaus, ill. V. Lee, Stan.
VI. Thomas, Roy. VII. Gillis, Peter.
VIII. Title.
PN6728.H8K7   741.5′973   81-10021
ISBN 0-516-02413-2   AACR2

THE INCREDIBLE HULK

We *do* mean "incredible!" This towering giant stands seven feet tall. He weighs half a ton. His powerful hands can crush through solid steel. His mighty legs can leap miles at a time. He can withstand any weapon any army can muster. He is unstoppable!

But who *is* the Hulk? Is he some rampaging, inhuman monster? Is he a tragically misunderstood mutant? Is he a hero?

THE MONSTER AND THE MAN!

The Incredible Hulk

Dr. Bruce Banner

He is all these things—and much, much more. The Hulk is the strongest living mortal on Earth. His rages are uncontrollable. He does not really want to smash and destroy. But he is always frustrated because he is always misunderstood. There is no place where the Hulk is accepted. There is no place where he can find peace!

And what of Dr. Bruce Banner, the man trapped inside the Hulk? Dr. Banner is one of America's most brilliant scientists. He invented the top-secret gamma bomb that first transformed him. Life and humanity mean everything to Bruce Banner. Violence toward his fellow men deeply disturbs him. Dr. Bruce Banner is a peace-loving man.

And peace is all the Hulk really wants, too. He wants to be left in peace. Unfortunately, people never leave well enough alone. Some villain shows up to try to take control of the Hulk. Or people who see him attack because they fear him. Finally, he is left with no choice— the Hulk lashes out!

And how!

But there is another side of the Hulk. He may be a slow thinker, but in his own way he is as much a humanitarian as Dr. Banner. When the Hulk sees an innocent person being hurt by some evil, it makes him mad. And when the Hulk gets mad, he fights back. No matter how many times some people attack the Hulk, he never turns his back on those who truly need him.

Before we continue, let us go back to the beginning. Back to that momentous event when a man became a monster. . .and a *legend*!

THE HULK

HALF-MAN, HALF-MONSTER, THE MIGHTY HULK THUNDERS OUT OF THE NIGHT TO TAKE HIS PLACE AMONG THE MOST AMAZING CHARACTERS OF ALL TIME!

BY— Stan Lee + J. KIRBY

PART 1

"THE COMING OF THE HULK"

5

6

11

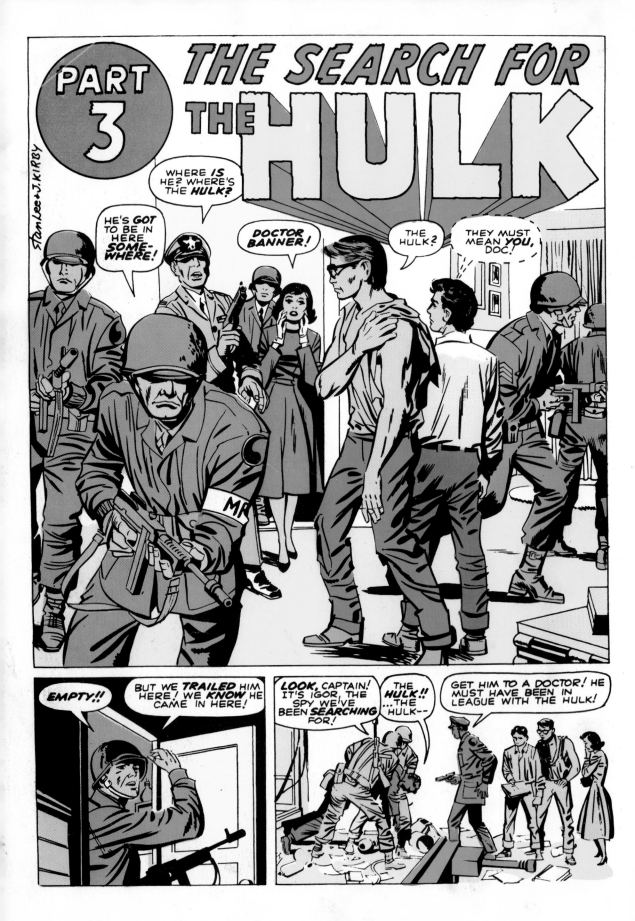

16

18

That was the beginning, just as it first appeared, way back in #1 of *The Hulk* comics magazine. Of course, a lot has happened since then. Shortly after that first story, Dr. Banner created a machine that allowed him to change at will. That would have been just fine—if it had continued to work. Unfortunately, after a number of such changes, the Hulk/Banner's body chemistry shifted. And then Bruce Banner could no longer control the changes in his body. Whenever sudden danger or emotional stress speeded up Banner's pulse rate, he changed into the Hulk. And it could happen at any time—not only at night. That's the way it is to this day.

Eventually, of course, the world found out that Bruce Banner and the Hulk were one and the same. After all, it was hard for Banner to hide the fact that he turned big and green in times of stress. Someone was bound to notice!

Since then, the world has had to weigh the threat of the Hulk against the value of Dr. Banner's brilliant mind. As you will see, the United States government goes to great lengths to keep Bruce Banner "free" of the Hulk. But when the Hulk starts tearing things up, they go for the big guns.

Life has not been all bad for the Hulk. He has had some good moments. He has made a few friends and allies along the way. (You might wonder why he doesn't have *more* friends. It seems to us that it would be a whole lot safer to have the Hulk as a friend than as an enemy!) Some of the Hulk's supporters were introduced in the first story. Let's take a closer look at them, as well as some others you might not know.

You met Rick Jones. He is the teenager who played such an important part in the Hulk's origin. Because Bruce Banner saved him from the gamma rays, Rick will always be loyal to the Hulk. Eventually, though, Rick realized he couldn't be with the Hulk at all times. As the Hulk grew more and more unpredictable and uncontrollable, he also began roaming. But, no matter how different their fates, Rick will never forget the debt he owes to Bruce Banner—and, thus, to the incredible Hulk.

Another important person you met was Betty Ross, the general's daughter. Betty came to care deeply for Bruce Banner. When she finally found out that he was the Hulk, she tried to accept it. She did feel compassion for the man-monster. But she could not overcome her fear. It would be a lot to ask of anyone!

The Hulk has had some super-powered friends as well.

Betty Ross

General "Thunderbolt" Ross

Captain America
The Wasp
Iron Man
Rick Jones
Thor
Giant-Man

THE AVENGERS!

The Avengers are a team of the world's mightiest Super Heroes. You will meet them briefly in the last story in this book (Ah! Ah! No peeking ahead!) Actually, it was because of the Hulk that the Avengers came together.

A certain villain was trying to get at Thor, the mighty thunder god. The villain started tearing things up. He made the destruction look like the work of the Hulk. So, naturally, Thor went after the Hulk. And so did several other heroes. Among them were Iron Man, Giant-Man, and the Wasp. But very soon these heroes discovered that the Hulk was innocent.

These heroes had worked so well together that they decided to become a permanent team. And, for a short while, the Hulk stayed with them. However, the Hulk had an unpredictable nature. He soon felt confined by the others and struck out on his own again.

About this time, the Avengers took Rick Jones under their wing. Rick even ended up fighting alongside the legendary Captain America for a while. But he always remained true to the Hulk.

AND THE DEFENDERS!

Although you won't meet them here, we thought you might like to know about the Defenders. This Super Team is one of the strangest ever formed. All of its members are outcasts in some way: Doctor Strange. The Son of Satan. Ghost Rider. Nighthawk. Hellcat. All are a little bit different—from each other and from everyone else! All are people who could not find acceptance in the outside world. It is little wonder, then, that the Hulk could find some comfort with this group.

Still, the Hulk really prefers to be alone. The world is just too confusing for him, so he tries to avoid contact with people as much as possible.

But there is another reason why the Hulk doesn't have many friends. It is a sadder reason. Many of those rare people who have accepted the Hulk as he is have been taken away from him. Sometimes, because the Hulk is too powerful to fight against, a villain gets at the Hulk through his friends. Sometimes, while trying to protect the Hulk from a frightened world, a friend is in the wrong place at the wrong time. Many are caught by some attack that the Hulk himself might easily survive. But they cannot survive.

So the Hulk avoids making friends. The loss hurts too much. Even this big, green, bad-tempered monster has a heart!

The following tale will give you a taste of the kind of action for which the Hulk is famous. The story begins on a happy note. Bruce Banner is about to marry Betty Ross. At the time, he thought he had been *cured*. He believed he would never again change into the Hulk. As it turned out, however, he was wrong.

But old Greenie doesn't have much time to mope around...

ONLY BRIEF HOURS AGO, THE COOL, SCIENTIFIC MIND OF *BRUCE BANNER* RULED AT LAST SUPREME OVER THE BROODING, BRUTISH *HULK*...AND HE STOOD AT THE ALTAR, ABOUT TO MARRY THE *GIRL HE LOVES!* BUT THEN STRUCK THE REVENGE-MAD *LEADER*...AND NOW THE *MONSTER* HAS TRIUMPHED ONCE MORE OVER THE *MAN*...!

DON'T REMEMBER... DON'T REMEMBER *ANYTHING!*

HULK ONLY KNOWS THAT HE WAS *HELPLESS* ...HELD PRISONER BY THE MAN CALLED *BRUCE BANNER!*

BUT, NO ONE WILL *EVER* CAPTURE THE HULK *AGAIN!*

NO ONE!!

...AND NOW, THE ABSORBING MAN!

STAN LEE EDITOR • **ROY THOMAS** WRITER • **HERB TRIMPE** ARTIST • **SAM ROSEN** LETTERER

23

25

28

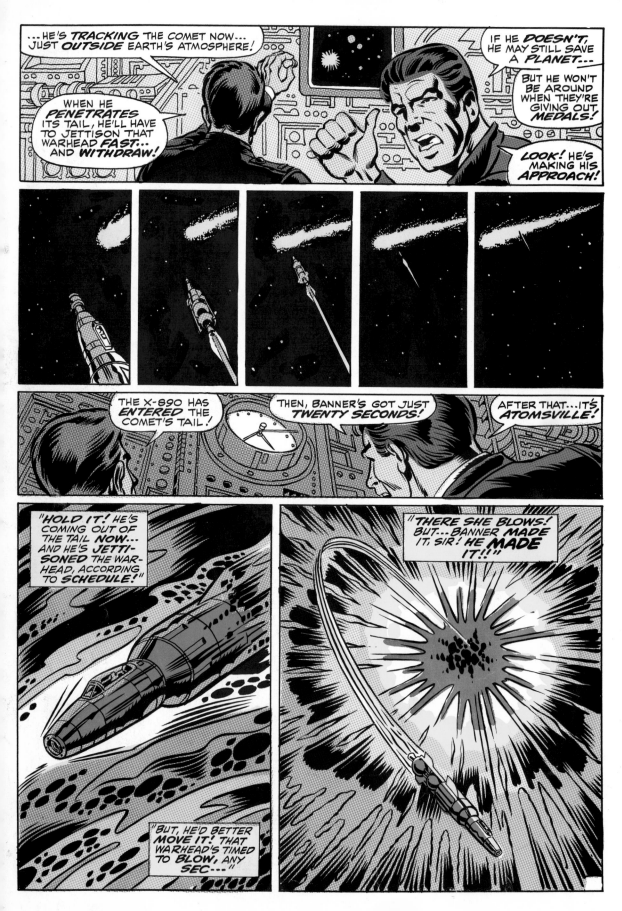

30

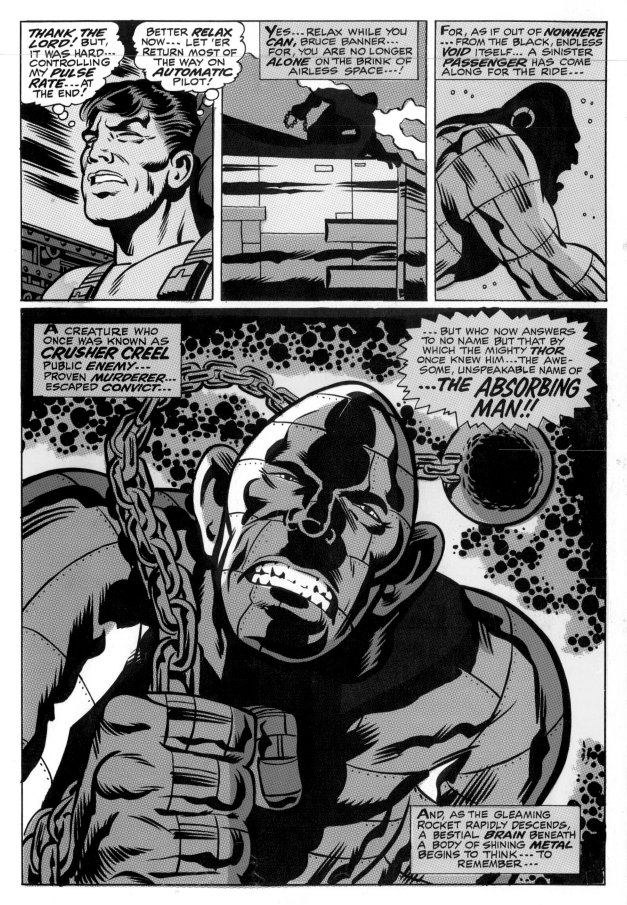

31

32

BUT THEN, BEFORE ANOTHER *WORD* CAN BE UTTERED --- OR ANOTHER *BLOW* BE STRUCK ---

SHROOOM!

WHOEVER THAT METAL MAN WAS, HE'S *DEAD* NOW!

THAT BLAST WOULD HAVE KILLED *ANYBODY* --- ANYBODY BUT THE *HULK!*

WHAT --??

YOU'RE AS STUCK ON YOURSELF AS THAT BLASTED *THUNDER GOD,* GRUESOME!

AND *YOU* AIN'T EVEN GOT A NUTTY *HAMMER* TO BACK UP YOUR BLUFF!

NOW, YOU JUST *PASS OUT* LIKE A GOOD LITTLE BOY, AN' I'LL ...

HUH?

YOU'RE LIKE *ALL* THE HULK'S FOES!

YOU FIGHT BETTER WITH YOUR *MOUTH* ... THAN WITH YOUR *FISTS!*

HULK DOESN'T TALK AS *PRETTY* AS SOME --- OR AS *MUCH* AS MOST ---

BUT HE CAN *FIGHT* BETTER THAN *ANY!!*

THWUMP!

NO, YOU *AIN'T*... 'CAUSE YOU'RE SO *STUPID* IT'S DOWNRIGHT *FUNNY!*

OTHERWISE YOU'D HAVE FIGURED OUT THAT I *WANTED* YOU TO TOSS THAT ENGINE MY WAY...

SO I COULD ABSORB THE *ENERGY* IT WAS STILL *RADIATIN'*...

...AN' BE ABLE TO DO... *THIS!!*

SKR NN CH!

HE STUCK HIS *HANDS* INTO THE GROUND... AND THE EARTH IS *MELTING*...

...MELTING ALL AROUND HULK'S *FEET!*

HULK IS... *SINKING*... CAN'T EVEN *JUMP*...!

THIS IS THE WAY IT *HADDA* END, CREEP...

...FROM THE MINNIT YOU TANGLED WITH THE *ABSORBING MAN!*

SO... AT LAST, HULK KNOWS... THE *NAME* OF THE ONE HE FIGHTS!

BUT, THAT WON'T *HELP* HULK...

...AS HE *SINKS* INTO THIS RED-HOT MUD... DEEPER, *DEEPER!*

MUST *THINK* OF SOMETHING... SOMETHING THAT WILL *SAVE* HULK...

BUT, IT'S ALWAYS SO *HARD*... SO HARD TO *THINK*...!

GIVE IT UP, GREENIE! YOU *AIN'T CUT OUT* FOR IT!

The Absorbing Man began his evil career by fighting another Marvel hero—the mighty Thor. Crusher Creel is pretty tough. And he keeps coming back. He survived the fate you just witnessed and returned for a rematch or two.

The Hulk has faced many powerful villains in his time. Let's take a closer look at some of them.

The deadliest, most truly evil foe that the Hulk has ever faced is the man called the Leader. The Leader is also a gamma-ray mutant. But gamma rays affect each person differently. They turned the brilliant Dr. Bruce Banner into the dull-witted Hulk. They gave the Leader one of the world's most amazing minds. Unfortunately, that mind is almost completely evil. The Hulk and the Leader have fought many times. Each time, the Leader seems to get closer to destroying the Hulk.

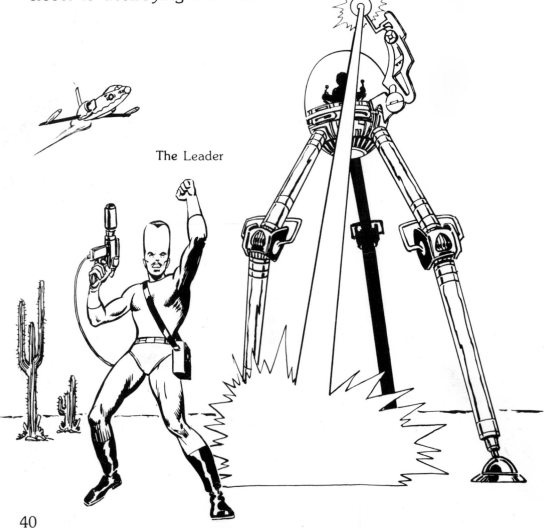

The Leader

One other foe of the Hulk's was created in a gamma-ray accident. One day a spy was nosing around Bruce Banner's lab. He turned on a machine that bathed him in gamma rays. The shocked spy was transformed into the Abomination. The Abomination is as powerful as the Hulk—but he also is able to think clearly.

The Abomination

Not all of the Hulk's foes are gamma-ray mutants. In fact, his foes come from nearly anywhere. A good example is the evil Tyrannus. He is the fanatical ruler of a kingdom deep inside the Earth. But he is a ruler in exile. He was banished centuries ago by the wizard Merlin. Now Tyrannus wants the entire world at his feet. Luckily, those feet keep tripping over the Hulk!

Tyrannus

The Hulk also has tackled an array of aliens from other worlds. He has even fought Super Villains who usually fight other Marvel Super Heroes! The Absorbing Man, as we now know, is a Thor villain who took on the Hulk. Another of the Hulk's foes is the Rhino, who is a Spider-Man villain. The Hulk has been under the Earth and on far-distant worlds. But no matter what the odds, it seems that, truly, nothing can stop the Hulk!

If the Hulk is ever stopped, it probably won't be at the hands of some mere Super Villain. There is one man who has made a career of trying to stop the Hulk. He was introduced in the very first Hulk story. That man is General "Thunderbolt" Ross, Betty's father. General Ross heads up the secret Hulkbuster Gamma Base.

PROJECT GREENSKIN
PROPOSED SITE OF MOBILE COMBAT FORCE ONE

Gamma Base

THE HULKBUSTERS!

Gamma Base was created by the United States government. Its main purpose is to capture and hold the Hulk. The Hulkbusters have succeeded in capturing him several times. But they have *never* succeeded in holding him—at least not for very long. Another purpose of Gamma Base is to study the Hulk. The Hulkbusters want either to control the man-monster or find a way to cure Bruce Banner permanently.

For these purposes, General Ross has at his disposal a full army, as well as some of the country's top scientific minds. Ross's army is equipped with many special weapons. They have been designed with the Hulk specifically in mind. But the Hulk keeps getting away!

Strangely, the Hulk and General Ross are alike in one way. No matter how hopeless the odds seem, both keep on going. Both keep hammering away. They are sure that *everything* has its breaking point.

Chances are, if anyone is ever able to stop the Hulk, it will be General "Thunderbolt" Ross and the Hulkbusters of Gamma Base!

Now we'd like to present one of the most unusual Hulk stories you are likely to read. Not only is the story unusual —it also will give you an inside look at one of the special functions of Gamma Base. You will see some of the ways the staff tries to *help* the Hulk.

This story features another gamma-ray character—Doc Samson. Though Doc Samson has become as powerful as any of the Super Heroes, he *is* a doctor. And that remains his first concern. Doc Samson now works with Gamma Base in the hope of curing the Hulk.

Read on, Hulk fan—you're in for a treat!

Caught in the heart of a *Nuclear Explosion*, victim of *Gamma-Radiation* gone wild, *Doctor Robert Bruce Banner* now finds himself transformed in times of stress into seven feet, one thousand pounds of unfettered *Fury*—the most powerful creature to ever walk the earth—

Stan Lee PRESENTS: THE INCREDIBLE HULK! ™

THE MONSTER'S ANALYST

THERE WAS A TIME WHEN DR. LEONARD SAMSON WAS ONE OF THE MOST RE-NOWNED *PSYCHIATRIC RESEARCH-ERS* IN THE WESTERN WORLD.

THAT, OF COURSE, WAS *BEFORE* HIS EXPERIMENTS WITH LIBIDINAL ENERGY AND CONTROLLED GAMMA RADIATION *TRANSFORMED* HIM INTO THE EMERALD-HAIRED STRONGMAN KNOWN AS *DOC SAMSON.*

THIS AFTERNOON, LEONARD SAMSON *RETURNS* TO HIS FIRST VOCATION.

JUST REMAIN *CALM*, HULK, THE IMPORTANT THING TO REMEMBER IS THAT WE ARE ALL YOUR *FRIENDS*--

--AND WE ALL WANT TO *HELP* YOU.

WRITTEN BY **ROGER STERN** (WITH AN ASSIST FROM PETER GILLIS) * ILLUSTRATED BY **SAL BUSCEMA** and **KLAUS JANSON** * lettered by JOHN COSTANZA colored by GLYNIS WEIN * SUPERVISED BY **BOB HALL**, EDITOR & **JIM SHOOTER**, EDITOR-IN-CHIEF

47

48

56

59

You can bet that the Hulk did *not* spend that week quietly at Gamma base! And you can also bet that the legend of the world's most unusual hero will continue. The Hulk will keep on searching for the peace he may never find. The world will go on misunderstanding and hounding him.

THE HULK—STAR OF TV!

When Stan Lee first created the Hulk, he wasn't sure whether the public was ready for such a different idea. The Hulk was something new. He was a heroic monster! Whoever heard of a monster who was also a hero? In fact, the idea *did* take a little while to catch on. But when it did—wow!

Today the Hulk is more than just a star in his own Marvel comics magazine. He also has his own TV series. It's even possible that seeing the TV series made you want to read this book. If so, you may have noticed a few differences between the TV series and these stories. They are unimportant differences. Small changes often are made when something from one medium is translated into another. This is called "artistic license."

Today the Hulk is amazingly popular. Not only is he the star of his own comic book and TV series—but there are also countless Hulk toys and games. The whole world seems to be getting "Hulkified!" Maybe it's because we see ourselves in the Hulk. The world often seems too complex to understand. Or maybe we just like exciting yarns. Whatever *your* reason for liking the Hulk, you can be sure of one thing. The Hulk will be around for some time to come. Because—as the Hulk himself would say—*nothing* stops the Hulk!

NOW YOU KNOW...

If you've read through this book, you have almost as much information on the Incredible Hulk as the folks at Gamma Base. Can you provide answers for the following questions?

What happened to turn Dr. Bruce Banner into the Hulk?

At first, Banner turned into the Hulk only at certain times. What were those times?

Later, something else triggered these changes. What was it?

What is Bruce Banner's occupation?

What part did Rick Jones play in the Hulk's origin?

Who is General "Thunderbolt" Ross?

What is the name of his team at Gamma Base?

What happened to Rick Jones after he separated from the Hulk?

What teams of Super Heroes has the Hulk been a member of?

What was Betty Ross's role in Bruce Banner's life?

How many people know that Bruce Banner and the Hulk are the same?

Who is the Absorbing Man?

What kind of treatment did Doc Samson give the Hulk?

Got those? Well, here are a few bonus questions to keep your Hulk wits tuned!

How tall is the Hulk and how much does he weigh?

The Absorbing Man was formerly the villain of *another* Marvel hero. Which one?

What are the two purposes of Gamma Base?

Besides the Hulk, what other characters mentioned in this book were created by gamma rays?

What is the one thing that the Hulk wants more than anything else in the world?

Do you think he will ever find it?

THE MEN BEHIND THE HULK!

STAN LEE

Stan has been working in the comics industry for more than thirty years. In that time, he has become almost as well known as the countless characters he has created. Stan was the editor, art director, and guiding force behind the company that became Marvel Comics. In those early days, and during most of the sixties, Stan wrote nearly everything for Marvel. He was a major force in reshaping the way in which comics were done.

Stan writes an amazing amount of material. He created many well-known features, including the Fantastic Four, Spider-Man, the Avengers, Daredevil, Iron Man, and— of course—the Incredible Hulk!

Today, Stan is Marvel's publisher and creative director. He supervises the handling of Marvel Comics characters in other media, chiefly television and motion pictures. Naturally, that includes the ever-popular Hulk television series.

JACK KIRBY

Jack is nearly a legend among comic-book artists. From the very beginning, he worked closely with Stan to shape the special visual style of Marvel Comics. Like Stan, Jack has spent more than thirty years producing a mind-boggling amount of artwork and other creations. Jack has drawn nearly every Marvel character at some time or another, but his most famous features include the Incredible Hulk, Captain America, and the Fantastic Four.

ROY THOMAS

Roy was one of the first new writers to be discovered by Stan when Marvel came to have more titles than Stan could keep up with. Roy quickly became a star in his own right. Besides doing a long stint at the helm of the Hulk magazine, Roy is also the man who brought Conan the Barbarian to the world of Marvel.

HERB TRIMPE

Herb is known throughout Marveldom as the Hulk artist supreme. He has penciled the Incredible One for nearly ten years. At first, the Hulk was done by several different artists, but then Herb developed a special Hulk look for the magazine.

ROGER STERN

Roger is one of Marvel's newer writers, but he is already showing signs of becoming comicdom's next big sensation. Roger worked for several years on Marvel's editorial staff. Since turning to writing, Roger has already tackled some of Marvel's best-selling features—including the Hulk, Spider-Man, and Captain America.

SAL BUSCEMA

Sal is comicdom's most prolific artist. There is probably not a single Marvel character he has not rendered at one time or another in his career. He is noted for his dynamic art and his clean, punchy storytelling. Sal is also versatile. He is able to move from an all-out action tale to a more unusual story—such as the last story in this book.

KLAUS JANSON

Klaus is an artist with a very special style. He has worked in the comics field for nearly ten years. Klaus has spent much of that time creating fantastic artwork for both the Hulk and the Defenders.